Would you dare?

WOULD YOU DARE
WALK ACROSS NIAGARA FALLS?

By Siobhan Sisk

HOT TOPICS

Gareth Stevens
PUBLISHING

Please visit our website, www.garethstevens.com. For a free color catalog of all our high-quality books, call toll free 1-800-542-2595 or fax 1-877-542-2596.

Cataloging-in-Publication Data

Names: Sisk, Siobhan.
Title: Would you dare walk across Niagara Falls? / Siobhan Sisk.
Description: New York : Gareth Stevens Publishing, 2017. | Series: Would you dare? | Includes index.
Identifiers: ISBN 9781482458305 (pbk.) | ISBN 9781482458329 (library bound) | ISBN 9781482458312 (6 pack)
Subjects: LCSH: Niagara Falls (N.Y. and Ont.)--Juvenile literature. | Daredevils--Juvenile literature.
Classification: LCC F127.N8 S57 2017 | DDC 971.3'39--dc23

First Edition

Published in 2017 by
Gareth Stevens Publishing
111 East 14th Street, Suite 349
New York, NY 10003

Copyright © 2017 Gareth Stevens Publishing

Designer: Laura Bowen
Editor: Therese Shea

Photo credits: Cover, p. 1 (Nik Wallenda) Barcroft/Barcroft Media/Getty Images; cover, p. 1 (Niagara Falls) Steve Biegler/Shutterstock.com; cover, pp. 1–32 (background) Nik Merkulov/Shutterstock.com; cover, pp. 1–32 (paint splat) Milan M/Shutterstock.com; cover, pp. 1–32 (photo frame) Milos Djapovic/Shutterstock.com; p. 5 Javen/Shutterstock.com; pp. 8–9 DeymosHR/Shutterstock.com; p. 9 (inset) Pete Spiro/Shutterstock.com; p. 11 (top) Ronald Summers/Shutterstock.com; p. 11 (bottom) Igor Sh/Shutterstock.com; p. 13 (main) Andibrunt/Wikimedia Commons; p. 13 (inset) Editor at Large/Wikimedia Commons; pp. 15, 18, 19 (all) Hulton Archive/Getty Images; p. 16 DcoetzeeBot/Wikimedia Commons; p. 17 William England/Hulton Archive/Getty Images; p. 21 Jappalang/Wikimedia Commons; p. 23 David Welker/Getty Images Entertainment/Getty Images; p. 24 Flickr upload bot/Wikimedia Commons; p. 25 arindambanerjee/Shutterstock.com; p. 26 Amanda Haddox/Shutterstock.com; p. 27 Robman94/Wikimedia Commons; p. 29 AFP/Stinger/Getty Images; p. 30 Taxiarchos228/Wikimedia Commons.

All rights reserved. No part of this book may be reproduced in any form without permission in writing from the publisher, except by a reviewer.

Printed in China

CPSIA compliance information: Batch #CW17GS: For further information contact Gareth Stevens, New York, New York at 1-800-542-2595.

CONTENTS

Are You Ready?	4
Not Just One	6
Major Attraction	10
Barrels of Dares	12
On the Wire	14
More Crossings	20
Wallenda Walks	22
Success!	28
For More Information	31
Glossary	32
Index	32

ARE YOU READY?

Imagine stepping onto a wire more than 100 feet (30 m) high. A huge waterfall fills the air with thundering noise. Below you, water mixes, promising to swallow anything that falls in. Welcome to Niagara Falls! Do you dare walk across?

DARING DATA

Native Americans named the falls. *Niagara* means "thunder of waters."

5

NOT JUST ONE

Niagara Falls is one of the most beautiful sights in the world. It's found between New York State and Ontario, Canada. It's actually a **series** of waterfalls on the Niagara River. Thousands of tons of water pour over the falls each second!

MAP OF NIAGARA FALLS

UNITED STATES

CANADA

Niagara Falls State Park

American Falls
Bridal Veil Falls

Goat Island

Horseshoe Falls

Niagara River

DARING DATA

The island between the two largest falls is called Goat Island.

7

The largest part of Niagara Falls is known as Horseshoe Falls. It's about 2,200 feet (670 m) across and about 185 feet (56 m) tall. The American Falls is about 1,060 feet (323 m) across and about 190 feet (58 m) tall.

DARING DATA

The smallest waterfall, Bridal Veil Falls, is 56 feet (17 m) wide.

Bridal Veil Falls

Horseshoe Falls

MAJOR ATTRACTION

Millions of people visit Niagara Falls each year to **experience** its amazing sights and thunderous sounds. There are places in the United States and Canada to view the falls safely. However, the falls also draws **daredevils** who like to do **stunts**.

boat tour

DARING DATA

Niagara Falls is often called one of the "natural wonders of the world."

BARRELS OF DARES

Many people have gone over the falls hoping to become famous. Some rode in wooden **barrels**. Teacher Annie Taylor was the first that we know of, going over Horseshoe Falls in 1901. She lived! Others died during their attempts.

DARING DATA

A man named Bobby Leach broke bones in his face and knees going over the falls in a steel barrel—but he lived!

Annie Taylor

Bobby Leach

ON THE WIRE

Other daredevils were even bolder. They walked over the Niagara **gorge** on a **tightrope**! The first to do this was Frenchman Jean François Gravelet-Blondin in the summer of 1859. He used a rope 1,300 feet (396 m) long and 2 inches (5 cm) thick.

DARING DATA

French **aerialist** Jean François Gravelet-Blondin was called "the Great Blondin."

15

The tightrope was tied between a tree on one side of the Niagara River and a rock on the other. Blondin refused to use a net below him in case he fell. He only used a long pole for balance.

DARING DATA

In the 19th century, tightrope walkers were also called ropedancers and funambulists.

Blondin crossed the Niagara gorge successfully and repeated the feat several times. Once he crossed with a wheelbarrow and another time with a man on his back. He stood on his head. He even crossed with a sack over his head!

DARING DATA

Blondin crossed the Niagara gorge hundreds of times during his life!

19

MORE CROSSINGS

In 1876, Italian Maria Spelterini crossed the Niagara gorge—with peach baskets on her feet. She crossed again blindfolded. She crossed once more with her hands and ankles bound together! In 1896, James Hardy, just 21 years old, became the youngest aerialist to cross.

Maria Spelterini

DARING DATA

Hardy crossed the gorge 16 times during the summer of 1896.

21

WALLENDA WALKS

Doing stunts in Niagara Falls State Park was illegal for a long time. It was over 100 years before another person walked across Niagara Falls. Aerialist Nik Wallenda was allowed to attempt a walk across Horseshoe Falls in 2012.

DARING DATA

Wallenda came from a family of tightrope walkers.
His grandfather died after a fall from a tightrope wire.

While other daredevils walked over the Niagara gorge, Wallenda wanted to be the first to walk over the actual falls. He said he had wanted to walk over Niagara Falls since he was 6 years old! On June 15, 2012, Wallenda stepped onto the wire.

DARING DATA

Wallenda started walking on a tightrope when he was 2 years old!

25

Wallenda had walked on higher tightropes and longer ones, too. But this walk was different. He said, "If I looked down at the cable, there was water moving everywhere, and if I looked up, there was heavy mist."

DARING DATA

Wallenda used a steel cable 2 inches (5 cm) thick and 1,800 feet (549 m) long.

SUCCESS!

Wallenda couldn't even be seen on the Canadian side of the falls at first. However, about 30 minutes later, he stepped into Canada. Thousands cheered the amazing aerialist. Do you think you could do what Nik Wallenda did? Would you dare?

DARING DATA

Wallenda didn't want to walk with a net under him. However, he had to since the stunt was shown on TV.

THE AMAZING NIAGARA FALLS!

NIAGARA FALLS: 3 falls
water speed: 32 feet (9.8 m) per second
total water flow: 3,160 tons (2,867 mt) per second

AMERICAN FALLS
height: 190 feet (58 m)
length: 1,060 feet (323 m)

BRIDAL VEIL FALLS
height: 181 feet (55 m)
length: 56 feet (17 m)

HORSESHOE FALLS
height: 185 feet (56 m)
length: 2,200 feet (670 m)

FOR MORE INFORMATION

BOOKS

Stine, Megan. *Where Is Niagara Falls?* New York, NY: Grosset & Dunlap, 2015.

Van Allsburg, Chris. *Queen of the Falls.* Boston, MA: Houghton Mifflin Harcourt, 2010.

WEBSITES

A Daredevil History of Niagara Falls
www.history.com/news/a-daredevil-history-of-niagara-falls
Check out this timeline of daredevil stunts at the famous falls.

The Daredevil of Niagara Falls
www.smithsonianmag.com/history/the-daredevil-of-niagara-falls-110492884/?no-ist
Read more about the Great Blondin.

Facts About Niagara Falls
www.niagarafallslive.com/Facts_about_Niagara_Falls.htm
Discover much more about the falls and see some awesome pictures.

Publisher's note to educators and parents: Our editors have carefully reviewed these websites to ensure that they are suitable for students. Many websites change frequently, however, and we cannot guarantee that a site's future contents will continue to meet our high standards of quality and educational value. Be advised that students should be closely supervised whenever they access the Internet.

GLOSSARY

aerialist: someone who does feats in the air or above the ground

barrel: a round, usually wooden container with curved sides and flat ends

daredevil: a person who does dangerous things, especially in order to get attention

experience: to have something happen to you. Also, the thing that happens.

gorge: a narrow passage through land, especially a canyon

series: a number of events that are arranged or happen one after the other

stunt: an unusual or hard feat requiring great skill or daring

tightrope: a tightly stretched rope or wire high above the ground that someone walks on or does tricks on

INDEX

American Falls 8, 9, 30
Bridal Veil Falls 9, 30
Canada 6, 10, 28
Gravelet-Blondin, Jean François 14, 15, 16, 18, 19
Hardy, James 20, 21
Horseshoe Falls 8, 12, 22, 30
Spelterini, Maria 20
Taylor, Annie 12
tightrope 14, 16, 17, 23, 25, 26
Wallenda, Nik 22, 23, 24, 25, 26, 27, 28, 29